The Tale of
Ticky the Elephant

Written By

Students of the Rafiki Institute of Classical Education

Contributing Authors

Aderite Ndegeya, Bienvenu Kadeli, Josiane Uzamushaka,
Pricille Cyuzuzo, Sharon Mutoni, and Violet Nankunda

Illustrated By

Sheri Del Core

Layout By

Eric Jones

Edited By

Julie Jones

To all the hard-working students, teachers, caregivers, missionaries, day workers and staff of the Rafiki Village in Rwanda who daily give their all to make the world a more peaceful and joyful place.

"Ha-rooooo!" trumpeted Ticky as he stomped, snorted, and snarled his way through the bush.

Ticky was an elephant who lived in a game park in the country of Rwanda on the continent of Africa.

Ticky was as big as a bus with a trunk as long as a tree.

He wore a fine red cape with shiny gold buttons.

None of the other animals in the park wore a cape and Ticky was certain this made him not only BIGGER but also BETTER than all the rest.

Ticky liked to spend his days chasing and frightening the other animals, especially three little monkeys called Zee-Gee, Bee-Bee, and Co-Co.

Ticky loved to see the fear in their little eyes when he lifted his trunk, roared, and ran after them!

One fine and sunny day, Ticky spent his morning teasing and tormenting all the animals in the game park.

He zipped after the zebras,

hopped after the hippos,

galloped after the giraffes,

whooshed after the warthogs,

ran after the rhinos,

and leaped after the lions.

Next, Ticky went looking for the monkeys.

He found Zee-Gee, Bee-Bee, and Co-Co hiding in the branches of a tall, tall tree. "Ha-roooo!" Ticky roared as he stretched out his long, long trunk.

But he could not reach them. "Ha-rooo!" Ticky roared angrily. "I'll get you monkeys!"

"Eee-eee-eee, you can't get me!" cried Zee-Gee.

"Eee-eee-eee, you can't get me!" cried Bee-Bee.

"Eee-eee-eee, you can't get me!" cried Co-Co.

Ticky backed up to get a running start as the monkeys trembled in fear.

"Ha-roooo!" Ticky roared as his heavy feet stomped the ground sending up red clouds of dust.

Ticky ran faster and faster. The tree got closer and closer. The little monkeys held on tighter and tighter.

KA-BOOM!

Ticky's hard head crashed into the tree
and his big body fell to the ground.

The earth quivered, the tree shivered, and the little monkeys swayed wildly in the branches.

The bump on Ticky's head put him right to sleep. Ticky slept for a long, long time.

When he woke up he was filled with pain all over his big body. But that's not all. Ticky had pain in his heart.

Ticky felt sorry for all the mean things he had done to the other animals, but especially to Zee-Gee, Bee-Bee, and Co-Co.

Ticky wanted to do something to show the little monkeys that he was sorry. But what could he do? Ticky thought for a long, long time and then he had a BIG idea!

Ticky worked on his BIG idea
for many days.

When he was finished, Ticky went to find
Zee-Gee, Bee-Bee, and Co-Co.

The monkeys were terrified when they saw Ticky coming until they noticed something different about him.

He was not wearing his fine red cape with the shiny gold buttons. He was not running and roaring. He was walking slowly, his head bowed humbly, and in his long, long trunk he was holding a gift box.

"My dear friends, please gather around," said Ticky. "I want first to share my heart and then to share my gift." Very timidly the monkeys came near. Ticky set the box on the ground and asked, "May I have your forgiveness for all the mean things I have done?"

The monkeys argued among themselves until finally they all agreed to forgive Ticky. "Come and open your gift," said Ticky.

Zee-Gee, Bee-Bee, and Co-Co slowly opened the box. "EEEEEE-EEEEEE!" they exclaimed, jumping up and down. Inside the box were three little red capes.

The monkeys put the capes on, hugged Ticky and began to dance and play on his long trunk.

From that day on Zee-Gee, Bee-Bee, and Co-Co had great peace because Ticky, who had been their enemy, was now their friend.

All the animals in the park lived together happily and joyfully, especially Ticky, who never chased the other animals again.

About This Book

This story was birthed on a sunny school-day morning in the summer of 2016 in a classroom in Rwanda. Students attending the Rafiki Institute of Classical Education (RICE) wrote this story along with their substitute teacher, Julie Jones, who was serving as a short-term missionary with the Rafiki Foundation. The assignment in the RICE curriculum was to write a "naughty animal" tale in the style of *The Tale of Peter Rabbit*. With chairs placed in a circle, the students contributed ideas as their teacher recorded the story.

This story would not be a picture book without the wonderful, whimsical illustrations done by artist Sheri Del Core. Sheri generously donated her time and talent to bring Ticky, Zee-Gee, Bee-Bee, and Co-Co to vibrant life.

All proceeds from the sale of this book will be donated to the Rafiki Foundation. To learn more about the work of Rafiki in Africa, visit www.rafikifoundation.org.

To God be the glory!

Made in the USA
Columbia, SC
10 February 2024